# Dancing with Dziadziu

SUSAN CAMPBELL BARTOLETTI

*illustrated by* ANNIKA NELSON

HARCOURT BRACE & COMPANY
San Diego New York London
Printed in Singapore

I remember when my grandmother was round as a loaf of bread and my arms couldn't fit around her waist. Now Babci's fingers are cold, and the bones float inside her skin.

"Dance for me, Gabriella," Babci says. "Show me your recital piece."

She has seen my snowflake a hundred times, but each time she pretends it's new.

"You're such a good snowflake," she says when I'm done. "You melt just right."

I don't melt just right, even though I practice more than any-one else in my class. My toes won't listen to my head, especially when my arms have to flutter.

Babci hums snatches of a song. "That's the polonaise your grandfather and I used to dance to. Have I ever told you about Dziadziu?"

She has. Dziadziu died before I was born, but I want to hear about my grandfather again.

"Every Saturday night, we danced," she says. "Polka, mazurka, polonaise. I wore the flowered skirt and the black velvet vest Mama made for me. How she pricked her fingers sewing those colored beads! My hair was braided, and I wore a halo of ribbons and flowers. Your grandfather said my eyes were robin-egg bright."

Her eyes close, and I wait by the bed. The only sound is the whisper of her breathing.

"I was just thinking about my papa," she says. "I was a little girl when Papa brought us over from Poland. On that ship, there were five hundred of us stepping on each other's toes. We ran out of food, and Mama traded her prize tea set for a few potatoes and a hunk of salty pork."

Babci has told me the story a hundred times, but each time I pretend it's new. "How awful," I say.

"Not so awful," says Babci. "Mama said we were lucky. Others didn't have a tea set to trade for food."

She drifts to sleep. I tiptoe from her room.

Mom is kneading dough at the kitchen table. "Why are you making Paska bread?" I ask. "Easter isn't for two months."

Mom's hand brushes her cheek, leaving it streaked with flour. "Well, Gabriella, Babci says she won't be here for Easter." Mom punches at the dough. "She wants Easter tomorrow."

So I dye the eggs and help Mom prepare the ham, kielbasa, horseradish, and lamb butter for the Easter basket.

When I check on Babci, she's humming low, so low I can hardly hear her. Her feet are moving beneath the blanket. "Have I told you about the chickens?" she says.

A hundred times, but I sit by her. "Tell me again."

"We lived in the coal patch, you know," says Babci.

I picture the rows of ramshackle houses along the stone streets of Shanty Hill.

"All the families raised chickens," Babci says. "We couldn't afford fences, so they flocked together — like one big polka. Nobody could tell the chickens apart."

"What did you do?" I ask.

"We painted their feet blue! Poor things always looked cold. Why, I can remember those chickens — "

Babci sniffs. I sniff, too. The warm, sweet smell of Paska bread has curled through the hallway and into the room.

"Just like Mama used to make," says Babci. "Every Monday she baked fifteen loaves in our brick oven. She carried them into the house on a big wooden board balanced on her head."

Babci squirms beneath the blanket and pulls it up to her chin.

"Are you cold?" I ask.

She makes a face.

"We warmed our beds with bricks from the fire. On a cold night, Mama gave us two bricks. On Saturday nights we took baths in a washtub in front of the kitchen stove." Babci chuckles. "Mama always let me use the water before my brothers."

I always laugh when I imagine Babci in a washtub.

"I went with Mama to pick coal at the slag pile. It was my job to crack the coal."

She shoos me away. "I'm tired, Gabriella. Let me sleep now."

On Sunday Babci wants to look pretty for her Easter dinner. I unpin her hair and let it fall past her shoulders.

"Braid it," says Babci. "Like I used to do for you. Do you remember?"

I remember. As I braid, Babci hums pieces of the song again.

"Tell me about Dziadziu," I say.

"After the dance, we walked the long way home," she says. "We stayed late on the porch, drinking lemonade. My brothers hid by the railing and teased us. When Papa came to the door, I had to go in. I knew your grandfather wanted to kiss me, but Papa always watched from the doorway."

"Too bad!" I say.

"Not so bad," says Babci. She leans close and whispers. "Your grandfather stole plenty of kisses. Ah, he looked so handsome in his white shirt."

Babci's eyes grow wet. I know she wants to see Dziadziu in his white shirt again.

Mom carries the Easter basket full of food into Babci's room. The priest has come for a special visit and joins us for dinner.

Babci doesn't eat much, but she smiles the whole time.

After dinner I dress in my ballet costume. "Did I ever show you my snowflake?" I ask.

"Show me again," says Babci.

As I flutter my arms, I suddenly see Babci, a little girl standing tiptoe on a crowded ship. My toes point, and Babci's painting the feet of chickens. I turn and she and Dziadziu are stealing kisses.

I know my grandmother will soon be dancing with Dziadziu again, but for now, her eyes are robin-egg bright for me.

"You're such a good snowflake," she tells me for the hundredth time.

And this time, I know I've melted just right.

Library of Congress Cataloging-in-Publication Data
Bartoletti, Susan Campbell.
Dancing with Dziadziu/Susan Campbell Bartoletti; illustrated by
Annika Nelson. — 1st ed.
p. cm.
Summary: A young girl shares her ballet dancing with her dying grandmother and the grandmother shares
memories of her family's immigration from Poland and of dancing with the girl's grandfather.
ISBN 0-15-200675-3
[1. Grandmothers — Fiction. 2. Polish Americans — Fiction.]
I. Nelson, Annika, ill. II. Title.
PZ7.B2844Dan 1997
[E] — dc20 95-47964

First edition
A C E F D B

The illustrations in this book are hand-colored linoleum cuts
printed on Daniel Smith archival printmaking paper.
The display type was hand-lettered by Georgia Deaver.
The text type was set in Centaur by Thompson Type, San Diego, California.
Color separations by Bright Arts, Ltd., Singapore
Printed and bound by Tien Wah Press, Singapore
This book was printed on Nymolla Matte Art paper.
Production supervision by Stan Redfern and Ginger Boyer
Designed by Lisa Peters

*For Mom and Dad,*

*with love*

*—S. C. B.*

*For Grandma and Oma*

*—A. N.*

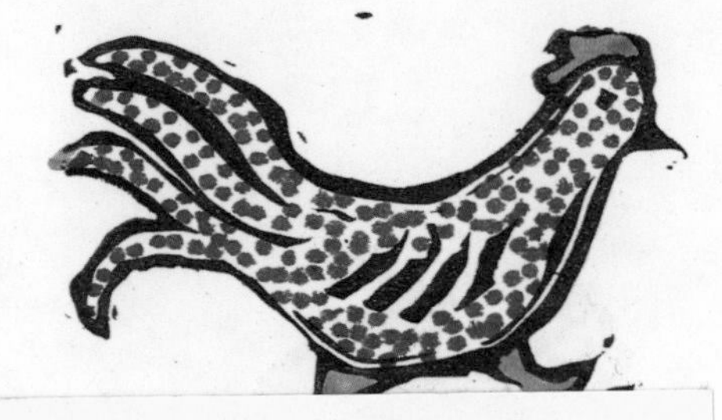

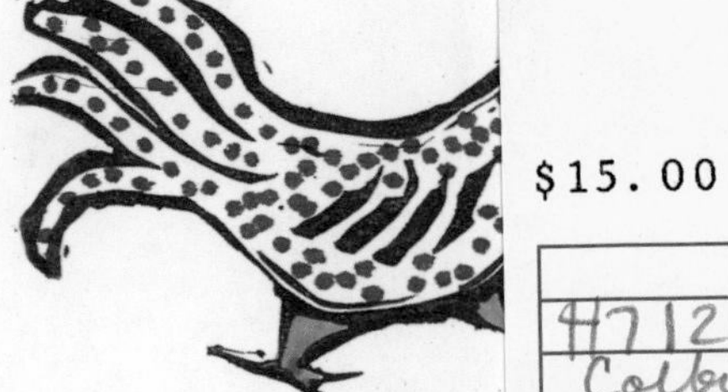

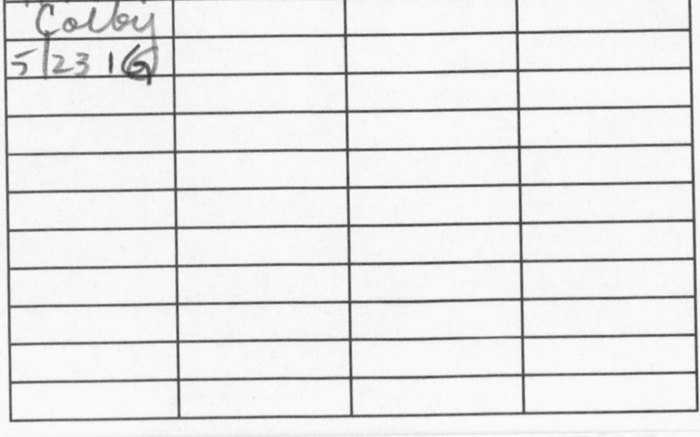